ai Or

oa Oa

or Ai

ie J

j Ee

ee Ie

Big, fat raindrops
dripped and plopped.

Drip, drop, plip, plop!
Listen!
“Listen!” moaned Goat.

"It's just rain," groaned Horse.

Tap, tap, tap!
Listen!
"Listen!" cried Goat.

"It's just Magpie," groaned Foal.

“Listen, listen!” cried Goat again.

"It's just Toad's clock," croaked Frog.

At ten, Goat fell asleep.

Goat snored. Goat snored a lot.
ai, ee,
ie, oa!

Horse, Foal, Magpie, Toad, and Frog jumped.

“Is it a foghorn?” cried Foal.

"It's just Goat," groaned Magpie.